Max Spaniel

BEST IN SHOW

David Catrow

Orchard Books
An Imprint of Scholastic Inc.
New York

For Larry, Mo, and Squirrelly — D.C.

Library of Congress Cataloging-in-Publication Data is available.
ISBN 978-0-545-05749-3
Lexile® is a registered trademark of MetaMetrics, Inc.
12 11 10 9 8 7 6 5 4 3 2 1   12 13 14 15 16/0
Printed in the U.S.A. 40
This edition first printing, January 2013

My name is Max.
I am not a dog.

I am a famous star.

My cool cousin Spaniel L. Jackson
was a big star.

When I get dressed,
I have to look the part.

Wrong.

Wrong.

Awesome!

Today I am getting ready for the big show.

I can act sad.   I can act mad.

I can act funny and wild!

There are many dogs in the show,

but there is only one me.

The show begins.

Spot hangs ten.
Fifi tries a swan dive.
Buster does a belly flop.
I dive —

for sunken treasure.

The barking contest begins.

Buster howls.
Fifi yips.
Spot woofs.

Anyone can bark like a dog.

I quack like a duck

and roar like a lion.

It's time for the talent contest.

Fifi wears a hat.

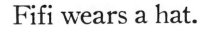

Buster sits.

Spot shakes.

It is my turn, so I make shadow puppets.

I'm pretty good at it.

The judge says,
"Let's start the music contest."

Spot starts to swing.
Buster plays the strings.
Fifi keeps the beat.
The judge taps his feet.

And I start to sing.

Buster, Fifi, and Spot bowwow.

And I just bow.

We all get a prize.